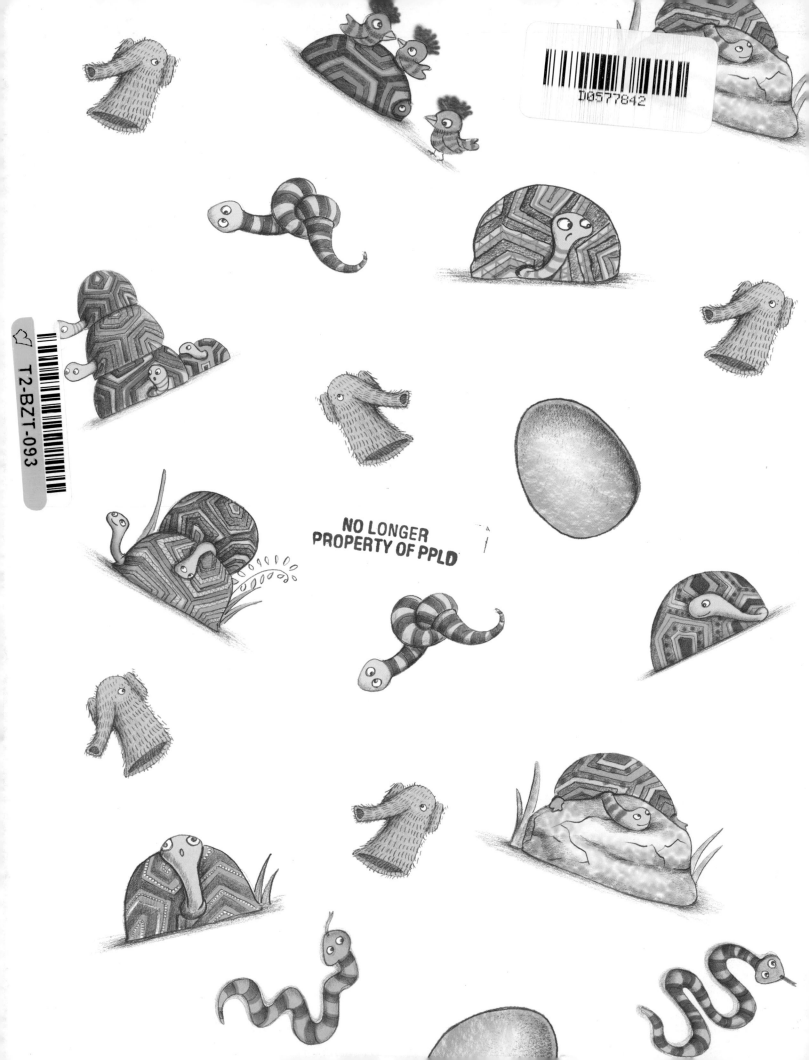

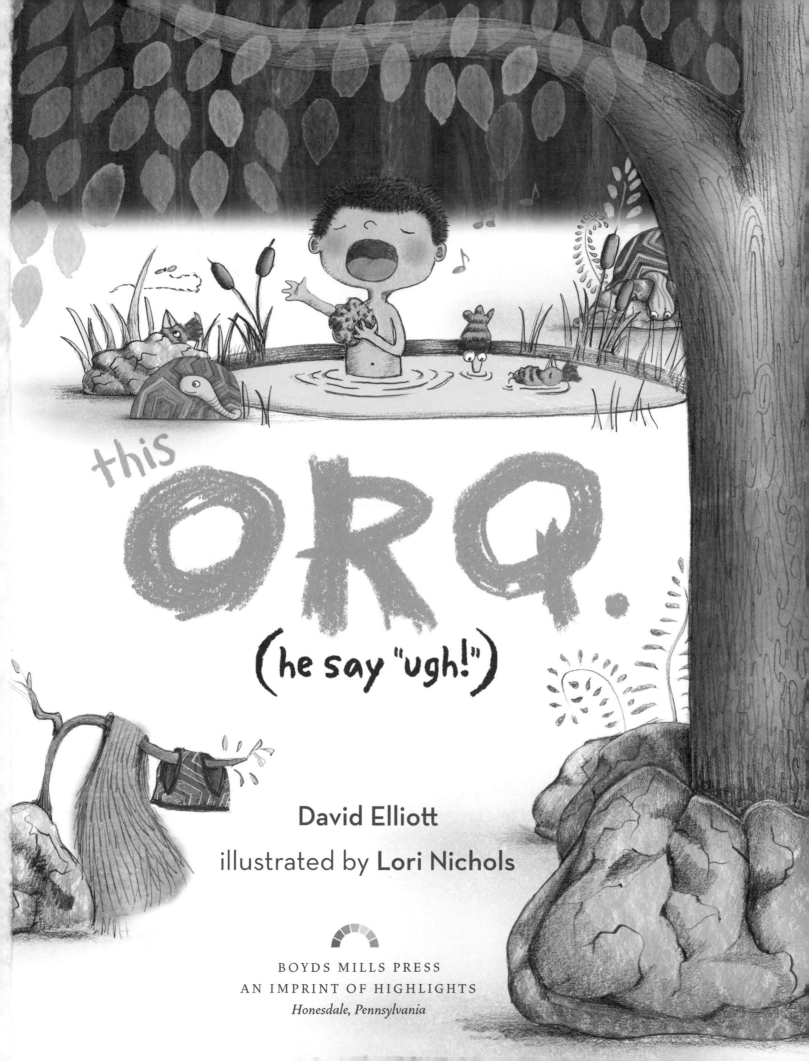

this ORQ.

(he say "ugh!")

David Elliott

illustrated by Lori Nichols

BOYDS MILLS PRESS
AN IMPRINT OF HIGHLIGHTS
Honesdale, Pennsylvania

## The Turtle Challenge

**How many turtles did the artist paint for this book?**
**The answer is on the back flap. (Hints: In each turtle-fort,**
**find the turtle with the number on it;**
**it will tell you how many turtles are on that page.**
**Don't forget the turtles on the jacket.**
**The "tremendous turtle" counts, too!)**

*This for Rebecca M. Davis.*
*David say "Fab!"*
—DE

*For Prentiss.*
*He top-notch friend.*
*He fun.*
—LN

Text copyright © 2015 by David Elliott
Illustrations copyright © 2015 by Lori Nichols
All rights reserved
For information about permission to reproduce selections from this book,
contact permissions@highlights.com.

Boyds Mills Press
An Imprint of Highlights
815 Church Street
Honesdale, Pennsylvania 18431

Printed in China
ISBN: 978-1-62091-789-3
Library of Congress Control Number: 2014958541

First edition

Designed by Anahid Hamparian
Production by Sue Cole
The text of this book is set in Neutraface.
The illustrations are done in #4 pencil on Strathmore drawing paper and colorized digitally.

10 9 8 7 6 5 4 3 2 1

This Orq.

He cave boy.

Wear skins.

No shoes.

Sometimes say . . .

**"UGH!"**

This Woma.
Best friend.

Every day
have fun.

But cave life tough.

Cold cave.

Dark night.

Raw bison.

And . . .

. . . DORQ!

Dorq big!     Orq small.

Dorq hairy!

Orq . . . ?

Caba no prize either.

Dorq!
**UGH!**

Caba!
**DOUBLE UGH!**

Orq's mother give advice.
"If you ignore them, sweetheart,
they'll stop bothering you."

That easy for *her* to say.
Dorq impossible to ignore.
Caba even worse.

Orq catch lunch.
Dorq eat lunch.

Woma find egg.
Caba take egg.

Orq and Woma build fort.
Dorq and Caba *like* fort.

Dorq and Caba mean!
Orq and Woma . . .

. . . fast!

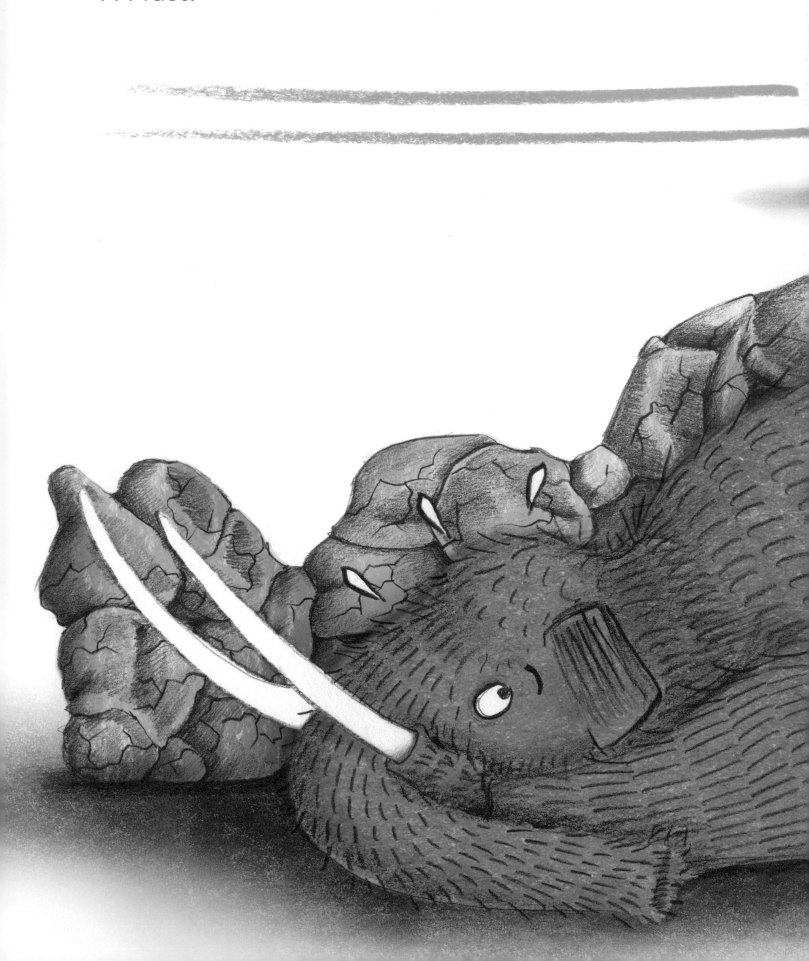

One day, Orq and Woma hunting.

Hunt big beetle.

Hunt large lizard.

Hunt
tremendous
turtle.

Find . . .

. . . Dorq and Caba!

Orq and Woma fast . . .

. . . but not fast enough.

Dorq!
# UGH!

Caba!
# DOUBLE . . .

# Now Orq angry.

This rock Dorq.

This rock Caba.

# BANG!

Oh.

Orq discover

# FIRE!

Orq Woma's hero.

Orq everybody's hero.

Warm cave.

Night light.

Bison burgers!

# YUM!

**DOUBLE YUM!**